MEG comes to SCHOOL

for Rebecca

MEG comes to SCHOOL

by Helen Nicoll
and Jan Pieńkowski

PUFFIN BOOKS

The first lesson was swooping and pouncing

WHOOSH

The bell rang for dinner

They all had different food

Mole
in the hole

Shrew
stew

Owl was top in soaring

middling at hovering

good
at
diving

and
bottom
in
swimming

It
was
Sports
Night

Owl
was
anxious

Meg
brought
Mog
to watch
the
School Sports

Everybody
noticed
Meg's hat

Owl won the night flight race

Goodbye!